T0130386

HEROES
TURBO-MAN
MIKE LANE

AuthorHouse™
1663 Liberty Drive
Bloomington, IN 47403
www.authorhouse.com
Phone: 833-262-8899

Interior Image Credit: Mike Hampton

This book is printed on acid-free paper.

ISBN: 978-1-6655-3351-5 (sc)
ISBN: 978-1-6655-3352-2 (e)

Print information available on the last page.

Published by AuthorHouse 07/29/2021

authorHOUSE®

LONG AGO TURBO-MAN KNOWN AS SCOTT AUSTIN, USE TO BE A BOXER. HE WAS A TEENAGER AT 17.

96
OH, HI THERE
HEY WHAT'S YOUR NAME KIDO?
THEY CALL ME SCOTT
THE RAIZER BLADE AUSTIN IN BOXING, BUT YOU CAN JUST CALL ME SCOTT.
I'M MEAGAN... SO ARE YOU AH MAN, OR POWER-MAN?
WELL I GUESS I'M AH LITTLE BIT OF BOTH AS YOU CAN SEE.

SOON AS MEAGAN AND SCOTT LEFT A TURBO METEOR HITS HIGH SCHOOL CENTRAL HIGH!!
I'LL SEE YOU AFTER CLASS!
ALRIGHT SEE YOU THEN MEAGAN!
BOOM!!!

YES IT IS REALLY THE CHOSEN ONE..?
AM I DEAD?
NO YOUNG SCOTT AUSTIN
WHERE AM I?
YOU'RE IN MY WORLD RIGHT NOW... THE WORLD OF MUTANTS, TITANS, ANG HUMAN MUTANTS AS WELL.
WILL I'LL BE ABLE TO RETURN BACK HOME TO MY PARENTS?
YES YOU WILL AS A HALF HUMAN, AND MUTANT TITAN WITH ABILITIES..

HOLD UP I THINK I HEARD SOMETHIN OR SOMEONE DAT IS...!

WHO OR WHAT IS DAT?!
ANYBODY DARES TO CHALLENGE ME OR STOP ME WILL DIE!...

HOW IS IT GOING STACY?
I'M DOING OK, I MEAN THINGS COULD BE BETTER BUT I CAN'T COMPLAIN.
15 YEARS LATER.

AS I GET READY
FOR A BATTLE
AND RETURN...!

ENNGH!

I'M YOUR WORST ENEMY YET.
EUGH!

EUHH!!! YOU'RE GOING DOWN NEXT!! UH!

YOU HAVE BEEN DEFEATED TURBO-MAN BY ME, WAR-NOC FOOL.

...WE SURE ARE SHORT TODAY ON STAFF..
YES I KNOW STACY
MR. ANDERSON, I NEVER THOUGHT DAT WE'LL BE...
I'LL BE HERE.. HOPEFULLY... REALLY I'M NIGHT SHIFT MANAGER BUT I'LL BE HERE.

MY TURBO SENSES ARE TELLING ME SOMETHINS AGAIN!!!
I SEE AH BETTER FUTURE AND UH BETTER LIFE

YOU SURE YOU WANNA WORK THIS SHIFT SCOTT?
I MEAN I DON'T WANNA GIVE YOU UH HARD TIME OR PUT MORE PRESSURE ON YA...
IT'S OK STACY.
YES I'M SURE THIS TIME... YOU'RE NOT GIVING ME ANY PRESSURE

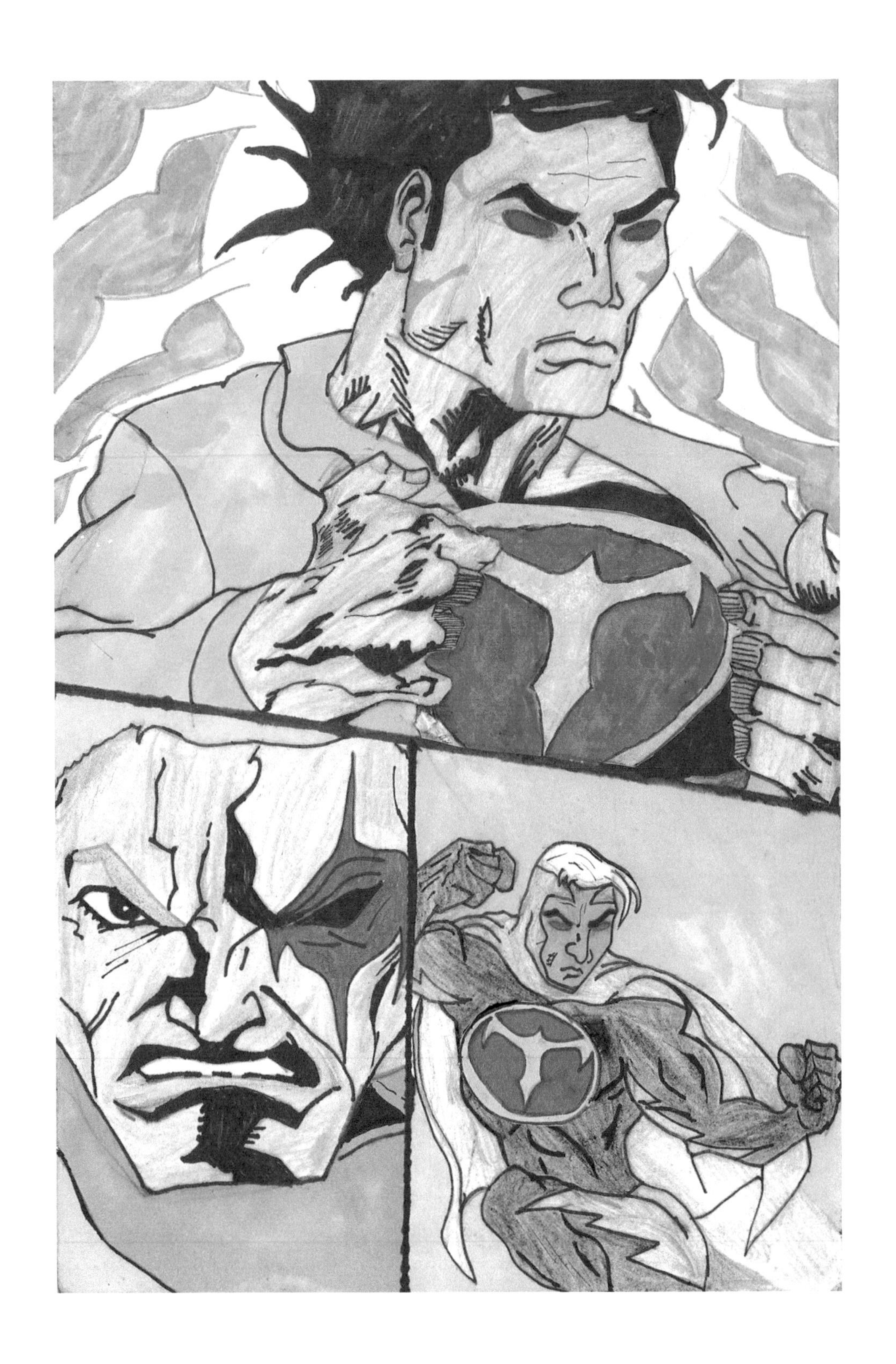

TH TRAIN!

I'VE SEEN WORST. BUT THE WORST HAS NOT ENDED ITSELVES.

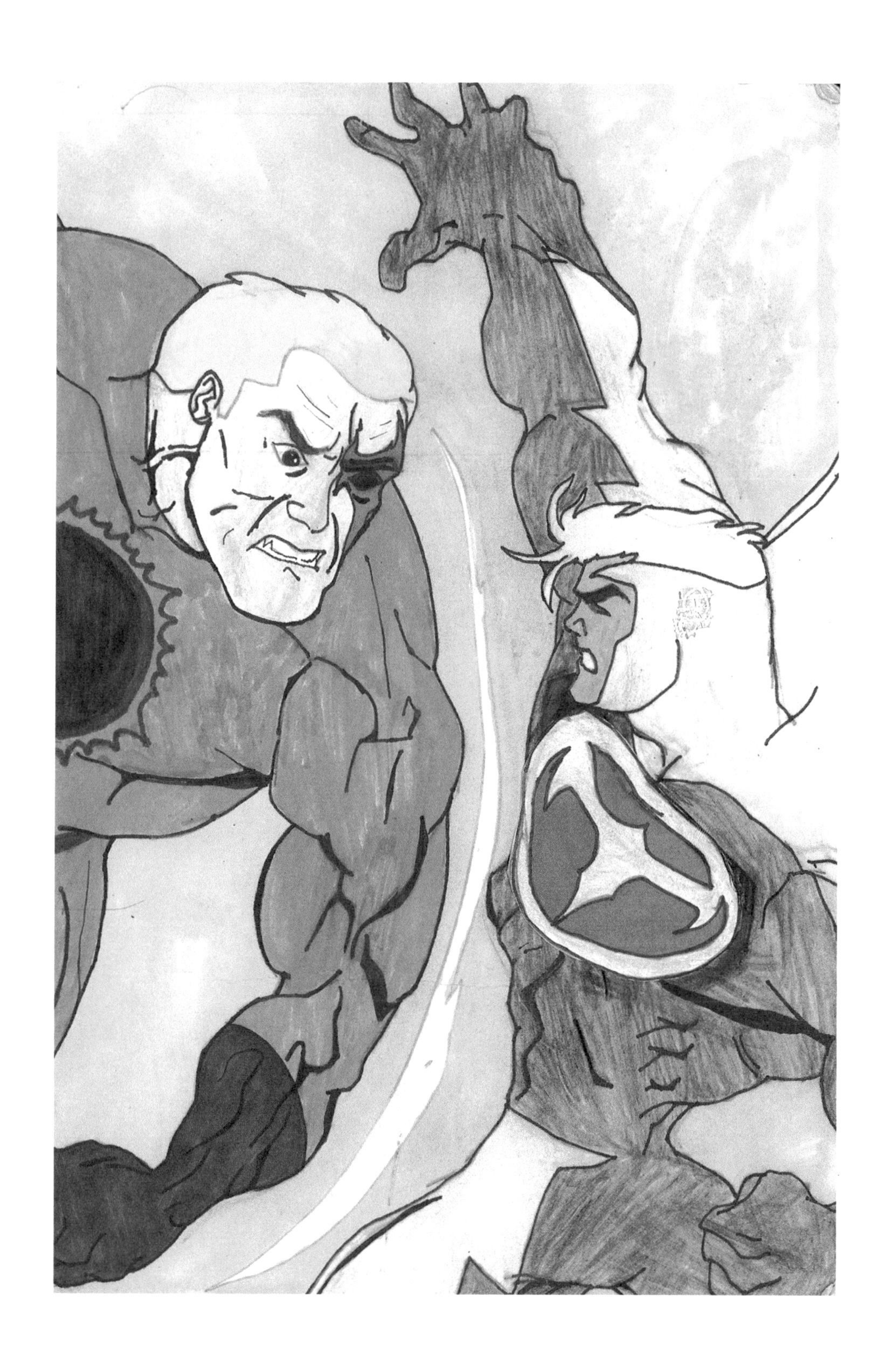

MY TURN!
AHHUH!!!

ONLY I CAN KILL YOU TURBO MAN!

EAEAHH!!

AND SO FINALLY THE EVIL WAR-NOC WAS DEFEATED AND THE WORLD IS IN GOOD HANDS FROM EVIL...FOR NOW...!

WE'LL MEET AGAIN! THIS IS NOT THE LAST FIGHT!!

AND THERE WILL BE TOO!..

I JUST CAN'T BELIEVE MY EYES ON WHAT I SAW
IS DIS REALLY TRUE OF WHAT I'M SEEING??...

IT'S TIME FOR ME TO PUT AN END TO YOU ONCE AND FOR ALL..WAR!!
YOU ARE GONE WAR!!
BOOM
UUUHHHHH!!! YOU'RE GOING DOWN TURUUU!!!

LONG WEEK THIS HAS BEEN. "I HOPE THAT I DEFEATED WAR!..."
I WONDER WHERE IS SCOTT AND EVERYBODY ELSE AT...? ALREADY AT AH NEW BEGINNING...

FINALLY THE TRIALS FOR THIS CASE IS CLOSED...

IT IS MORE PEACEFUL THEN IT SEEMS...NOW. AH NEW WORLD AND A BETTER DAY.

WELL, GOOD MORNING THERE SPORT.

GOOD MORNING STACEY...

WELL SCOTT IT'S GOOD TO SEE YOU BACK NOW...

JUSTICE WILL BE SERVED BY THE GOOD OF GRACE

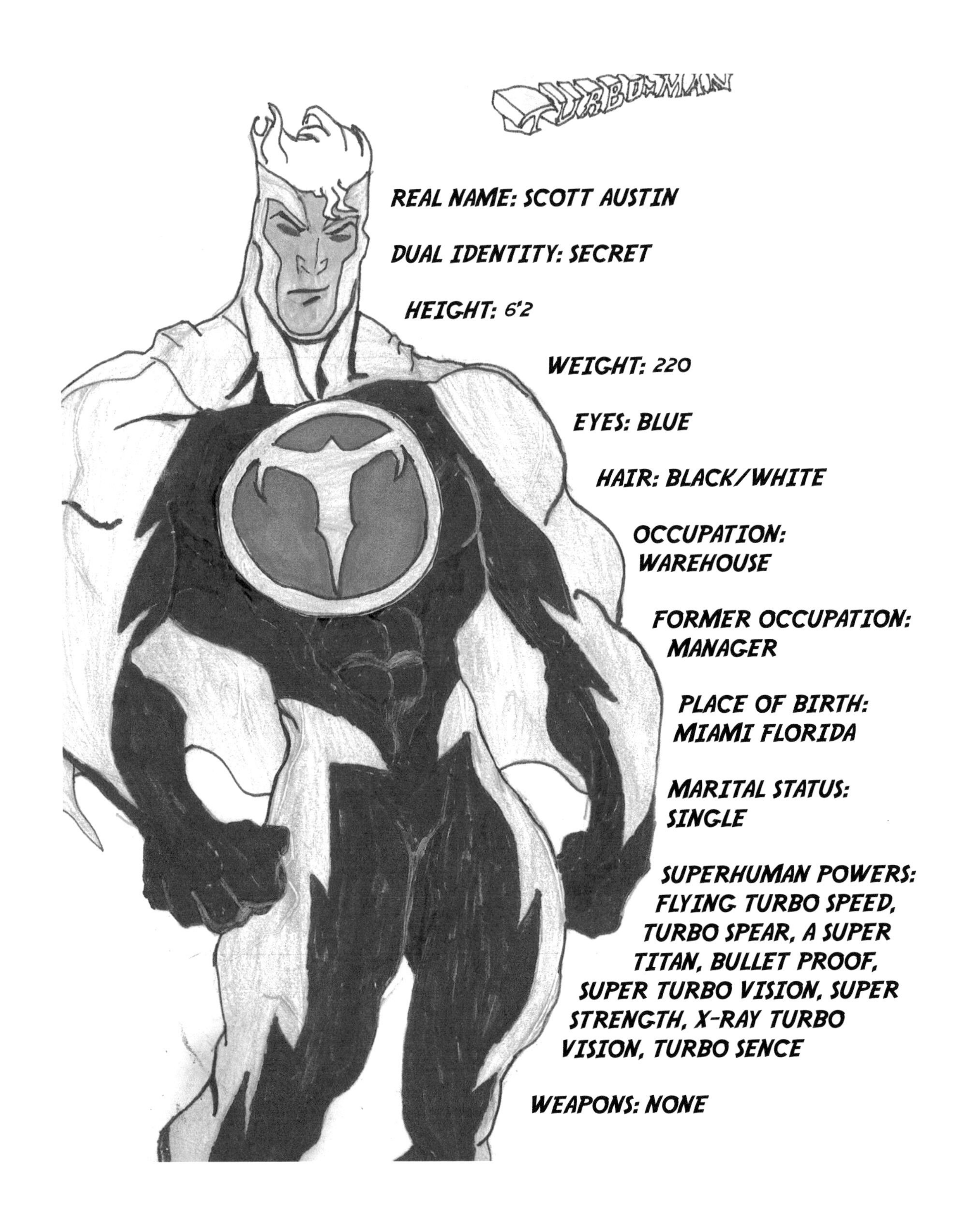
TURBOMAN
REAL NAME: SCOTT AUSTIN
DUAL IDENTITY: SECRET
HEIGHT: 6'2
WEIGHT: 220
EYES: BLUE
HAIR: BLACK/WHITE
OCCUPATION: WAREHOUSE
FORMER OCCUPATION: MANAGER
PLACE OF BIRTH: MIAMI FLORIDA
MARITAL STATUS: SINGLE
SUPERHUMAN POWERS: FLYING TURBO SPEED, TURBO SPEAR, A SUPER TITAN, BULLET PROOF, SUPER TURBO VISION, SUPER STRENGTH, X-RAY TURBO VISION, TURBO SENCE
WEAPONS: NONE

Printed in the United States
by Baker & Taylor Publisher Services